The Christmas Cottage

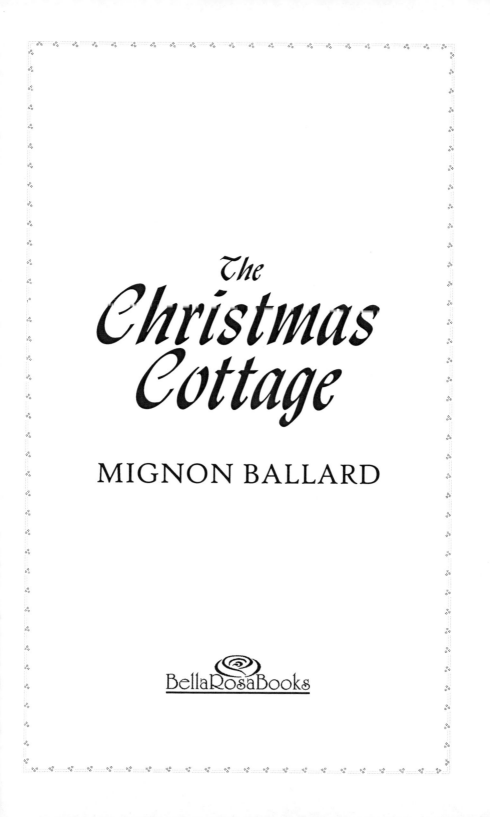

The
Christmas Cottage

MIGNON BALLARD

BellaRosaBooks

BellaRosaBooks

THE CHRISTMAS COTTAGE
ISBN 978-1-933523-22-4

First printed: October 2007

Library of Congress Control Number: 2007937987

Printed in the United States of America on acid-free paper.

Cover and interior art by Joyce Wright – www.artbyjoyce.com

Book design by Bella Rosa Books

BellaRosaBooks and logo are trademarks of Bella Rosa Books

10 9 8 7 6 5 4 3 2

For my sister, Sue Marie, who was born on Christmas Eve, and for all those who love Christmas—and even those who don't. Embrace the joy!

Chapter One

It was happening again.

Christmas had turned its back on her. And she, it. At the airport, strangers laughed and chatted with one another before boarding separate planes for family and home. Arriving passengers were hugged, kissed, and sometimes even cried over, then rushed away in a happy frenzy. No one was there to meet her.

Beaming carolers sang of reindeer, angels, joy to the world. Merry felt no joy, only the fear

1

that lay like a lump of dirty snow beneath her heart. Maybe it would have been easier if she didn't love Christmas so. Wasn't she born on Christmas Eve? Meredith. Our own Merry Christmas gift, her mother had called her, and except for that time long ago, the holiday had always had a special significance for her.

When the call came that morning she had just taken her jam cake from the oven; its spicy aroma blended with the fresh green scent of the nine-foot fir that brushed the ceiling. Merry was ready for Christmas. Swags of evergreens scalloped the banisters, a wreath of pine cones surrounded a fat red candle on the table by the telephone. Merry picked up the tiny snow globe beside it and turned it as she answered, watching white flakes swirl over a miniature cottage.

After she replaced the receiver, Merry stood, still clutching the small globe, as if staring at it might make the awful news go away. Years ago she had bought the quaint little globe with the tiny cottage inside at a garage sale, and as always, it made her think of Lucinda.

Now the gladness of the season evaded her, but Merry couldn't escape from Christmas. Later at the hospital the fiber optic Christmas tree in the lobby mocked her in swirling colors of red, gold, and blue, and the receptionist wore a Santa hat that swung crazily over one eye. Even the nurses' station in the intensive care wing was festooned with plastic holly and Merry had to peer between two huge poinsettias to see the woman behind the counter.

Only a few short hours ago she had been getting ready for the holidays, putting last minute touches on her centerpiece, finding just the right candles for the table. Things she considered important. Now nothing mattered except that her husband of thirty-two years lay close to death in this Atlanta hospital. She had flown over three hundred miles from Greens-

3

boro, North Carolina, to be here, not knowing what she would find. *Just tell me—tell me now—is my husband still alive?* Merry couldn't bring herself to ask.

"Excuse me . . ." Her voice came out in a croak.

The nurse behind the counter frowned, studying someone's chart. "Yes? Can I help you?" She adjusted purple-framed glasses with one finger and clutched the chart to her chest.

"My husband . . . They called this morning and I came as fast as I could. Brian Enright . . . is he . . . ?"

"Oh, Mrs. Enright. I'm glad you're here." Her voice softer now, the nurse set the chart aside. "There's no change, I'm afraid. You can see him if you like, but only for a few minutes. The disease was caused by an internal infection so he isn't contagious.

"Now, don't be surprised if he doesn't respond. He's a very sick man." The nurse touched Merry's arm as she led her through the swinging doors to the intensive care unit.

Only a few days ago this man had laughed as he teetered on a ladder to top their tree with a star, galloped around the block pulling their two-year-old grandson in his wagon, sung tenor in the church cantata. Tonight he lay pale and restless, eyes closed, with tubes going into his body.

Now and then he tossed his head and moaned, and a sheet was tied to the railings of his bed to cover his body because, the nurse said, he couldn't stand the touch of fabric against his skin.

Merry covered his hand with hers. He didn't respond. She leaned down to lay her cheek against his and whispered his name. "Brian, I'm here, honey. I love—love—love you." She kissed his cheek, his forehead. "Don't you leave me . . . I need you. We have things to do, places to go."

Did his eyelids flicker? She couldn't be sure. "Christmas is almost here, and our new grandbaby's due any day—a girl this time. Won't it be wonderful to hold a baby again?" Merry pressed his fingers. "We have Little League games to go to, dance recitals—and don't forget the beach trip we planned!" They had already reserved a house for the whole family for a week in July. She couldn't imagine going there without him.

In spite of his illness, he was a handsome man. Brian's thinning hair was more gray now than sandy, and the laugh lines were deeper around his eyes, but his mouth, even in repose, looked as if it might break into the familiar wide smile.

He didn't. Merry sensed, more than saw, someone in the doorway behind her and turned to see her husband's nurse standing there. His name was Charles and he wore a green smock and a small gold ring in one ear. "He's holding his own," he said. "We're giving him the strongest antibiotic possible."

His manner was kind, but she knew by the sound of his voice that there was nothing more

6

they could do.

"When will we know?" she asked.

"If it's going to take hold we should know something by morning."

Charles waited while Merry stroked her husband's forehead. "I'll be close by," she said, kissing him once again. "See you in the morning." She tried to sound positive, upbeat, but this time she was glad he couldn't see her face.

"When can I see him again?" she asked Charles on her way out.

"You'll hear the doors buzz open at six in the morning," he said, "then the doctors make their rounds around seven. Dr. Pierpont should be able to tell you something then." He smiled and touched her shoulder. "Try to get some sleep," he said as she hesitated at the door. Merry wondered if she would ever see her husband alive again.

Seeing Merry's tears, Charles grasped her hand. "Hey, meningitis is treatable if we catch it in time—and he has one of the best neurologists around."

If we catch it in time.

A sweet-faced woman in the gray uniform of a hospital volunteer walked past, softly humming a carol: "Silent Night," Merry's favorite. At her smile Merry felt the tears well up and turned away. What good would tears do now?

The nurse with the purple-rimmed glasses, whose last name, according to her badge, was Luther, showed her to the waiting room. "There's a telephone in here," she said, "and restrooms and snack machines just down the hall."

The room was dark. Several people were asleep in recliners lining the walls. Others had shoved two chairs together to make a place to stretch out. In the light from the hallway Merry could barely make out an empty chair in the far corner and stumbled over legs and bundles to reach it. The luminescent dial of the clock on

The Christmas Cottage

the wall said it was 11:43.

The plastic cushion creaked as Merry sank into it and she let herself lean back and close her eyes. To her surprise the chair was comfortable and she spread her coat about her like a blanket and felt the gray leaden numbness seep from her middle into her head and limbs. But sleep wouldn't come. It was three days before Christmas, she was alone in a strange city, and she wasn't sure her husband was going to make it through the night.

Chapter Two

Meredith Enright couldn't have felt more alone if she'd been marooned on an island in the middle of the ocean. Her husband had been stricken while on a business trip, and the only name familiar to her in the whole city of Atlanta was that of the man who had spoken to her on the phone that morning—one of the many vice presidents of a large soft drink corporation, and Brian's newest client. Walker Langford. Merry had never met the man, although Brian had mentioned him from time to time. He had sounded young and frightened.

Brian had become so ill during a business luncheon, Walker said, that he had rushed him to the emergency room. Thankfully, while her husband was still capable of communicating, he had passed along his cell phone with his home number on automatic dial and it was soon after that she'd received the call. A little over an hour later Merry was just getting ready to leave for the airport when Walker Langford phoned again to tell her doctors had performed a spinal tap to confirm their suspicions of bacterial meningitis.

Brian had suffered recently with a severe sinus infection but it seemed to have cleared up and Merry assumed he was coming down with a cold when he complained of aching the day before he left on his trip.

"Why not postpone this until after the new year?" she suggested. "Nobody works this close to Christmas anyway."

But this was an important sale, and Brian, a manufacturer's representative for several computer companies, had wanted to close the deal so he could relax and enjoy the holidays. Their daughter Jan, and her husband and two children, who lived nearby would be joining them Christmas Day and Brian had been putting together a dollhouse for six-year-old Beth. He could hardly wait, he said, to see the expression on her face when she saw it.

Their son Carter and his wife Amanda lived several states away, and since they were expecting their first child in a matter of days, they would be unable to come. Neither of their children could join her to be with their father. There was no question of Carter's leaving Amanda this close to her due date, and Jan had two young children at home.

"Oh, Mom! I wish there were some way I could come with you!" Her daughter had cried when Merry told her of Brian's illness. "If I can find somebody to keep the children for a couple of days I can try to get a plane out tomorrow."

"This close to Christmas? Honey, don't even think about it. Just pray—pray for both of us, and I'll call you as soon as I know anything." Merry knew both their children would be with them in thought every waking minute, and the knowledge of it gave her strength.

But not sleep. A man on the other side of the room snored loud enough to shake mountains, the woman in the next chair reeked of some kind of sickening jungle scent perfume, and only fourteen minutes had passed since the last time Merry had looked at the clock. Plus, she was getting a cramp in her leg.

If I stay in this close little room one more minute, I'll go crazy!

Feeling like a drowning victim surging to the surface, she threw her coat about her, grabbed her belongings, and crept from the stifling room. Her appetite had deserted her and she had eaten little on the plane. Although she still wasn't hungry, Merry knew she should put something in her stomach or risk being sick herself. Hot chocolate would be warming if she could just remember where to find the snack machines.

From a room down the hall the television Ghost of Christmas Yet-to-Come threatened Ebenezer Scrooge, and two elderly women whispered together in the corridor. One of them pointed the way.

Red crepe paper bells dangled above the door of the snack room, and a small artificial tree decorated with strings of popcorn and jellybeans stood on a table along with containers of sweeteners and coffee creamer.

For a few seconds Merry thought of how clever it was for somebody to think of making a garland out of jellybeans, then wondered if the sticky sugar would attract ants. But what did it matter? What did anything matter now?

If anyone had asked Merry how the hot chocolate tasted, she wouldn't have been able to tell them, but it was moderately warm and she used it to wash down the half pack of cheese crackers that had become her supper.

A woman about Merry's age came in and selected a soft drink from the machine. The man who was with her (her husband, Merry presumed), hovered close behind her.

"That's loaded with caffeine," he said. "You won't close your eyes all night. I wish you'd go home and get some sleep."

The woman looked at the can as if she were memorizing it. She had dark circles under her eyes. "It wouldn't do any good," she told him. "Besides, I'd rather stay here—in case there's any change."

"Honey, you'll wear yourself out." He put an arm around her as they left, and Merry, unnoticed in the corner, felt even more alone. Walker Langford had kindly invited her to stay at their home, but Merry declined, saying she wanted to be near her husband.

"I wish I could keep you company at the hospital," he said, "but my wife's family is having their Christmas dinner tonight and I don't know how late we'll be." He insisted on giving her his phone number and asked her to call in the morning.

Merry looked again at her watch. It was a little after one—and almost five hours before she would be allowed to see Brian again. Maybe someone at the nurses' station could check on his condition.

Nurse Luther's shift was up, but a large woman with curly gray hair and snowman earrings said she'd see what she could find out. She had a cheerful scout-leader kind of voice and a nice smile, and earlier had allowed Merry to put her small suitcase behind the counter for safekeeping. Surely she would bring good news.

"I'm sorry, I'm afraid there's no change," she told Merry a few minutes later.

"Is there a chapel somewhere?" Merry had been praying since morning, but it should be quiet there, and private.

"I'll show you." The volunteer in gray stood

16

behind her holding an arrangement of ever-greens. She smelled of fresh pine and cedar. "I'm on my way down there anyway."

The chapel was a tiny room on the first floor with rows of pews on either side of a center aisle. The room was dim with only a soft light illuminating a small altar at the front. Merry took a seat about halfway down and closed her eyes. She thought of Brian lying helpless, and so removed from her world she couldn't even communicate with him. But she could love him; she could think of his sense of humor, his gentleness, the way he touched her face in passing, and how he liked raisin and peanut butter sandwiches. She thought of them taking long walks in the woods together, getting up in the night with sick children, taking time about sharing aloud passages from favorite books, and she sent those thoughts to him in her mind and in her heart. God would have to take care of the rest.

A Gideon Bible had been left in the pew,

but it was too dark to read. Merry tried to remember the Twenty-third Psalm; she had memorized it in Sunday school when she was nine and thought she would never forget it, but her head seemed to be filled with dryer lint. What came after *The Lord is my shepherd, I shall not want?* Something about oil, and green pastures—comforting words. *Yea though I walk through the valley of the shadow of death* . . .

Merry wasn't ready to walk through that valley, and she wasn't ready for Brian to walk through it, either. She thought then of the Christmas story, the story of a newborn baby who brought love—who *was* love—and hope. That night in the small, dark chapel Merry grasped at that hope as she began to repeat the familiar words from Luke softly to herself.

And there were in that same country, shepherds abiding in the fields . . . and it brought her peace.

Light sliced the room as the rear door opened and someone came and sat in the pew across from her. A woman. Someone like her,

18

someone who was aching, hoping. She wore the uniform of a volunteer—probably the Gray Lady who had been humming earlier, the one who had led her to the chapel, Merry thought. Now the woman knelt and bowed her head. Merry couldn't see her face, but she knew her heart.

Merry curled into the corner of the pew and closed her eyes. The pew smelled of lemon oil and the scent was fresh and strong as if it had been recently polished. Merry inhaled the citrus aroma. It smelled like Aunt Martha's house . . .

Chapter Three

Life couldn't get any better than this, Merry thought. It was the last day of school before the Christmas holidays, she would be spending the night with her best friend Ginny, and tomorrow she and her family were going to get their tree.

That was before their principal came to the door of her third grade classroom and held a long, whispered conference with her teacher in the hallway.

Merry, curious, glanced at the girl across

from her who giggled as she dipped a Santa sucker into a cup of punch and popped it into her mouth. They were having their holiday party and the room was littered with cookie crumbs and popcorn. Probably making too much noise, Merry thought, counting the chocolate kisses in her goody bag—a gift from Mrs. Dixon, their teacher.

"Meredith, would you come here for a minute, please?" Only moments ago, their teacher had been reading aloud from a funny story about an elf who ate too much candy. Now her voice had lost its cheer.

Merry's slight body felt too heavy for her legs as she walked to the front of the room. Had she been talking *that* loud? Louder than all the rest?

Mrs. Dixon was smiling, but it wasn't a real smile, and Merry knew the difference. What she saw in her teacher's face, made her want to run away and hide. Merry's mother had been hurt in an accident, Mrs. Dixon told her, and she should gather her belongings and wait in the school office for her father to come for her.

As Merry passed Ginny's desk, her friend reached out and touched her, and her eyes were dark and sad. "Oh, Merry, I'm sorry!" she said.

Merry couldn't answer. She knew her friend hurt for her, but it was Merry's mother who was injured, not Ginny's. Merry couldn't bear to think of her mother lying in the hospital all wrapped in bandages. She couldn't bear to think of going back to stay in a home without her mother in it.

And she soon found out she wouldn't. "Honey, your mother's in a coma," her dad said when he came to the school for her. "She's not conscious right now—doesn't respond to anyone, and the doctors don't know when she'll come out of it."

"I want to see her. When can I see her?" Merry asked. She knew if she could just kiss her mother, throw her arms around her and tell her how much she loved her, her mother would

22

start to get well.

"I don't think that would be a good idea just yet," her dad said. "Your mom's in a special room, and they'll let me in to see her for only a few minutes at a time." Her dad was a house painter, and when he stroked her hair, his hands were rough and smelled of turpentine and the strong soap painters use.

"Is she hurting much?" Merry grabbed her dad around the waist and cried into his stomach.

He gathered her into his arms. "No, honey. I don't think she is."

"But when can she come home?"

He scooped her small hands into his large ones and kissed them. "I don't know . . . I just don't know."

As they drove home the familiar sights along the way didn't seem the same anymore. The friendly brown dog who lived in the yellow house on the corner didn't run to the fence and wag his tail as he usually did when they passed

by. The magnolia tree in the yard next door
looked dark and sad. Its heavy limbs drooped to
the ground.

At home, Merry found her brother, Buddy,
in his room packing to stay with his friend Alex.
At eleven, Buddy thought he was too old to cry,
but his eyes were red and puffy and Merry could
tell he was trying to be brave. Merry would be
staying with their aunt Martha for a while, she
was told.

"But why can't I stay here with Ginny's
mom?" She asked her dad as he began to take
clothing from her closet and fold things into a
big suitcase.

"Merry, Ginny's family plans to drive to her
grandparents' for Christmas. They'll be leaving
in a day or so." Her dad sighed as he pulled her
into his lap. "I'll be spending most of my time
with your mother, and I need to be sure you're
being taken care of. Your mom would want to
know someone's looking after you—you know
that, don't you? And Aunt Martha's her own

sister; she'd rather you be with her." His eyes were begging her, and his voice sounded tired—like it had a great big crack in it.

Merry felt like she had a huge gash in her middle and that all her insides had leaked out. Her throat burned and her head ached from crying. "I want Mama," she said.

"I know you do, but right now I need you to be my brave girl," her dad said. His kiss felt cool on her warm forehead. "Your aunt Martha will be here soon."

Aunt Martha might be her mother's sister, but the two were nothing alike, Merry thought. Her aunt had never married, had no children, and worked full-time as assistant to the president of a large department store all the way on the other side of the Blue Ridge Mountains in Knoxville, Tennessee. She spared no expense on the gifts she gave Merry and her brother: the nicest clothes, the newest toys, even piano lessons, and Merry liked her fine, but Aunt Martha was always so *busy*. She never had time to play and never seemed to want to. Merry wondered if she ever had. And she lived in a house way out in the country past the edge of the city—so far back in the woods, Merry had never seen a neighbor. *I'll die of loneliness there! There's nobody to play with!* Merry thought, but the look on her dad's face stopped her from saying it.

The first thing Aunt Martha did was to repack Merry's suitcase—which was probably a good thing, Merry noticed, as her dad had forgotten to include any underwear. Before leaving, Merry went through the house to tell it goodbye. She ran her fingers along the smooth surface of the dining room table that her great grandfather had made of walnut trees from his own farm. In the center, a fat red candle squatted in a circle of feathery cedar and pine. The fresh scent made Merry think of a few days before when she went with her mother to collect them in the woods at the edge of town. In the kitchen, a cookbook lay open to a recipe for the spice cookies her mother always made to eat while they decorated the tree. Nuts and bright red apples filled a wooden bowl on the hearth, and boxes of ornaments waited by the living room window. Merry could hardly bear to look at the calico swag of fat pears and partridges that hung beneath the mantel. Her mother had made it a few years before from a pattern in a magazine.

Later, Merry sat quietly in the front seat beside her aunt holding a worn, stuffed clown on her lap. As she was leaving, her brother had given her a rare hug and pressed it into her hands. "You can have Jo-Jo," he said, "but be sure and bring him back." Until a few years ago, Jo-Jo had sat on her brother's pillow, but now lived in Buddy's closet because, Merry knew, he was ashamed for his friends to know he still cared about him. Buddy had smashed the clown so flat from sleeping with him, their mother had had to restuff him twice. Now Merry fingered the faded yellow ruffle around the toy's neck and it soothed her just a little. Raindrops splashed on the windshield and rolled away in crooked rivulets as they drove past familiar streets and out past the edge of the little North Carolina town where Merry lived. The raindrops didn't know what would become of them, Merry thought, and neither did she. Later, her aunt said, the rain might even turn to snow. But Merry didn't care.

It seemed to take forever to get to the outskirts of Knoxville where Aunt Martha lived, and it was dark when they arrived. During the drive, her aunt had talked with her, asked her about school, her friends, and—how was she coming along with the piano lessons? Merry answered, "Fine," to all of them. She wished Aunt Martha would leave her alone.

She was surprised when her aunt pulled into the parking lot of a restaurant before going to the house. "Your dad tells me you've hardly eaten a thing all day, and I could use a little something myself," she told Merry. "Let's get

28

out and stretch our legs and have some supper.
Tomorrow you and I can go to the grocery
store and you can tell me what you like."

She would like to go home, Merry thought.
She would like for her mama to be well and
strong again, but she let her aunt order a hamburger for her and a bowl of chicken noodle
soup. Merry ate most of the soup and the pickle
from the hamburger. When Aunt Martha asked
if she'd like some ice cream, Merry shook her
head.

"What happened to my mom?" she asked,
as her aunt sipped coffee.

"Her car was hit at an intersection. The
person coming from the other direction didn't
stop at the stop sign." Aunt Martha put down
her cup and took Merry's hand. "It wasn't your
mother's fault."

Merry didn't care whose fault it was. "But
what did it do to her? How did it hurt her?"

Her aunt looked down at her lap and Merry
didn't think she was going to answer. "She has

some broken bones, honey, and a concussion. Right now she's in a coma. Your mother's sleeping; she won't know anything for a while."

Merry sensed her aunt wasn't telling her everything. "But when will she come home? When will I see her?"

"I don't know, Meredith. I hope it won't be long, but sometimes a coma's not a bad thing. It lets the body heal."

Merry didn't think it sounded like such a good thing to her.

"Tell you what," Aunt Martha said. "When we say our prayers before we go to bed tonight, we'll pray for your mama together." She squeezed Merry's hand. "I love her, too, you know."

That night Merry prayed hard—harder than she had ever prayed in her life. She told God He could forget about the bride doll she'd asked for—even the new skates. She wanted to wake up at home in her own bed. She wanted her mother to come into her room and flap open the shades like she always did and say, "Rise, Merry, rise, and wipe your weeping eyes; fly to the east and fly to the west, and fly to the one you love the best!" She wanted it all to be a bad dream.

But the next morning she woke in her aunt's spare bedroom with Jo-Jo clutched to her face.

Chapter Four

That afternoon at the grocery store, Merry's aunt bought her two coloring books, the biggest box of crayons she could find, and a package of that sweet cereal her mom never allowed her to eat. Later, she even let Merry teach her how to play "Go Fish," but even winning wasn't any fun.

"One day this week, we'll have to see if we can't find us a Christmas tree," Aunt Martha said that night over supper.

The Christmas Cottage

A bite of potato felt like it had turned to rock in Merry's stomach, and she pushed pieces of ham around on her plate. She knew her aunt was trying to make her feel better, but the only tree Merry wanted was the one that would stand in their living room window back home.

And just before bedtime, her dad called to tell them her mother's condition was un-changed.

She cried so much in the bathtub, Merry was sure the water level rose at least an inch.

"These things just take time," her aunt said when she came in to hear her prayers. "It doesn't mean your mom's not getting better, honey." She sat on the side of the bed with an old book in her hands. It was one she'd loved as a child, she said, and if Merry liked, she could read some aloud each night.

Merry said, "Okay," not expecting to like it—but she did. It was about the Five Little Peppers who were very poor and lived in a little brown house with their mother—only the mother in the book was so nice she made Merry think of her own. She turned away so Aunt Martha wouldn't see she was struggling not to cry.

Merry's aunt waited until the next afternoon to tell her about Mrs. Boggs. It had started to snow around noon, and by the time it began to grow dark, white mounds covered the yard. Merry wondered if it was snowing at home. If only she were there, she and Ginny would go sledding on the hill behind her house or help her mom build a snowman in their yard. Last year her mother had created a tall, skinny snow statue of a man with a great big nose that looked a whole lot like Mr. Herman, the grouchy postman who left packages out in the rain. Her mother said it wasn't him, but Merry knew better!

She stood at the window watching the flakes swirl past and wondered what Buddy was doing now, and if Ginny had left for her grandparents'. Aunt Martha had put red candles on the mantel and arranged a carved Nativity scene she said had belonged to her grand-mother on the small table by the window. Now she brought a bowl of popcorn from the kitchen and set it on the floor by the gas fire. "Would you like to play some cards?" she offered.

"Could I go outside in the snow?"

"I'm afraid it's a little late now—almost dark, and it's freezing out there, Meredith."

"Then tomorrow—"

Her aunt didn't answer right away and Merry knew something not-so-good was coming. Whenever a grownup is quiet like that, you could be fairly sure they were trying to think of an easy way to tell you something you don't want to hear, she thought.

"Merry, you know I must go back to work tomorrow," her aunt began. "I dislike having to leave you, but this close to Christmas my job is especially demanding. I've asked a neighbor to come and stay with you. She lives just down the road and her name is Mrs. Boggs. I'm sure you're going to get along just fine." Aunt Martha smiled. "And then, of course, when I get home, we'll have supper together, and maybe you'll teach me some more card games— why, I'll bet Mrs. Boggs would like to learn some, too."

But Mrs. Boggs, Merry learned, wasn't interested in anything but knitting something out of ugly brown wool and watching television. She watched game shows in the mornings, soap operas in the afternoons, and whatever else she could find in between. And the monstrous brown thing grew larger and longer.

Aunt Martha's neighbor was a large, pasty-faced woman whose graying brownish hair was forever escaping from a wad at the back of her neck. She wasn't unkind or anything, she was just sort of *there*.

For lunch that day she gave Merry a bowl of

canned tomato soup and a peanut butter sandwich, and when Merry asked if they might make
some cookies or fudge, the woman replied that
she didn't want to mess up her aunt's clean
kitchen. After lunch, Mrs. Boggs went to sleep
in front of the television with her mouth open
and Merry drew a picture of her and enclosed it
in a letter to Ginny. She also wrote to her dad
and Buddy and colored half the pictures in her
Christmas coloring book.

When her dad called that night to ask how
she was, Merry wanted to tell him about boring
Mrs. Boggs and that she wanted to come home
so badly her stomach hurt, but she knew that
would just make him worry more. After all,
Aunt Martha couldn't help it if she had to go to
work.

Merry's mom was still the same, he said.
Was her mother never coming home? Was she
going to sleep forever? Or worse. But Merry
couldn't let herself think about that. Her aunt
had brought her a large, squishy teddy with a

red ribbon around his neck and three new puzzles to play with. She named the bear Stuffy, Jr., after a teddy she had loved when she was little. That night Merry slept with the bear on one side and Jo-Jo on the other and tried to pretend she was in her own bed at home. It didn't work.

Chapter Five

The next morning, Merry played with her puzzles and colored in the rest of her coloring book. For lunch that day, Mrs. Boggs served canned chicken noodle soup and a peanut butter sandwich. Merry wanted to make snow ice cream, but Mrs. Boggs said she didn't know how.

Later, just as Merry expected, the sitter settled down in Aunt Martha's big armchair, turned on the television to a silly show about all these people who didn't seem to like each other very much, and dropped off to sleep. Merry waited until the woman started snoring, then bundled herself into boots, coat, hat, scarf and mittens and stepped quietly out into the snow.

The drifts came way above her knees, and Merry made a deep pathway as she trudged through them, then, finding a level place in the backyard, began to shove and pack the snow into a heap to make a snowman. But it was harder than she'd thought, and the snow wouldn't stay where she had put it. It was no fun trying to make a snowman by herself! New tears icy on her cheeks, Merry gave the pile of snow a hard kick and sent it flying. She was getting ready to go back inside when something cold hit her just behind her ear and snow crumbled onto her shoulder.

Someone laughed, and she turned to see a child about her age standing at the edge of the woods. The person wore a bright blue knitted cap and matching mittens with a purple snow-

suit that covered most of her (or his?) body.
From where she stood, Merry couldn't tell if the
figure was a boy or a girl.

"Hey!" she called. "Stop it! Where—"

But before she could finish her sentence,
Merry was hit with another snowball—this time
in the stomach. "Okay, you asked for it!" Merry
yelled, and scooped up a fistful of snow to
return fire.

A blizzard of snowballs continued until
both children, laughing, tumbled to the ground.
"I'll give up if you will," her opponent said,
dumping snow from a bright yellow boot.

Merry did the same. "I didn't know
anybody lived near here," she said. "Where did
you come from?"

"Just down the trail . . . I'm Lucinda." The
girl pulled off her cap to shake the snow,
revealing a crown of soft ringlets as golden as
candlelight. Her cheeks were bright with cold
and her gray eyes were so warm and friendly,
Merry almost forgot about her freezing hands

and feet. "I'm Merry," she said, wondering why her aunt didn't tell her about someone her age living close by.

"What happened to your snowman?" Lucinda asked, examining the remains of Merry's attempt.

"Aw, I couldn't get it to stick. I've never made one by myself."

Her new friend banged snow from her mittens. "Then let's do it together! Let's make something different."

"Like what?" Merry asked.

"How about a snow elephant?"

"Why not?" Merry said, and the two of them began piling snow into a big fat mound.

The elephant, she found, was much easier to make than a snowman, and with the two of them working, it was soon almost finished. When they had trouble building the trunk, Merry found a curved limb which they covered with snow.

"We're packing the elephant's trunk!"

The Christmas Cottage

Lucinda said, laughing, and Merry giggled, liking the taste of the cold, sharp air in her mouth. She had almost forgotten what it was like to have fun.

"Let's go to my house for hot chocolate," Lucinda said as they stuck the stick "tusks" into place.

Merry peeked into the window. Mrs. Boggs was still dozing over her knitting. And after all, the woman hadn't told Merry she couldn't go out. Merry doubted if her sitter would even know she wasn't there.

"Let's!" she said, and raced after Lucinda down the snow-banked trail through the woods.

Chapter Six

Snow fell from the trees with soft little plops as they followed the winding pathway through a forest of gray and white. A small brown rabbit peeked at them from behind a log, and once Merry was almost sure she saw a fawn.

"We're almost there!" Lucinda said, darting ahead. "Race you!"

The air was so clear and so cold it hurt to breathe, kind of like when she ate ice cream too fast, and Merry was glad when they turned in at the gate of a small house set deep in the woods. If Lucinda hadn't shown her the way, she probably wouldn't have noticed the small brown cottage snuggled there against the snow-capped pines that embraced it. Why, it looked like the Five Little Peppers' house must have looked, she thought, and told her friend about the book her aunt was reading.

Candles glowed in the windows and a bright green holly wreath hung on the heavy oak door. The two girls wiped their feet before going inside, and Merry took a deep breath as she pulled off her mittens. The little house smelled of cinnamon and cloves, and of cedar from the big tree in the corner.

"You're just in time to help decorate the tree," Lucinda's mother said when Lucinda introduced her. "Why don't you take off those wet boots and get warm by the fire and I'll make us some hot chocolate?"

Lucinda's mother had soft brown hair that curled like Lucinda's did and her blue eyes crinkled at the corners when she smiled.

A calico cat dozed in front of the fire that crackled in a big stone fireplace and Merry held her hands to the blaze, feeling its warmth melting away some of the coldness inside her. The feathery tree in the corner almost touched the ceiling, filling the room with its fresh, woodsy smell, and a plump baby played on a pallet nearby.

"This is my little brother," Lucinda said, kissing the baby's toes to make him laugh. The baby reached up to touch Merry's face. He was the sweetest baby Merry had ever seen and she wanted to gather him close. She glanced at Lucinda.

"He wants you to hold him," Lucinda said. "It's okay; you can sit here and hold him on your lap."

While the two girls played with the baby, Lucinda's mother brought out a tray of hot chocolate and spice cookies along with bowls of popcorn and cranberries to string for the tree.

The Christmas Cottage

As they sat there with red and white garlands growing longer and longer, Merry told them about her mother, and although neither of them spoke, the expression in their eyes told her the news made them sad, too.

But the popping of the embers in the fireplace lulled her, and the cooing of the baby made Merry forget about sad things for a while. They had draped the last of the strings around the tree when Merry realized she had stayed much longer than she planned. Mrs. Boggs might've called the police by now, and her aunt would be worried sick!

"Oh, my goodness! I have to go," she said, struggling into coat and boots. "My aunt won't know where I am."

But Merry was relieved to find it wasn't yet dark when she stepped outside. At the door, Lucinda's mother stooped to kiss her lightly on the cheek. "Watch your step now," she said. "Lucinda will walk part of the way with you."

"Come back tomorrow and I'll show you a

great place to sled," Lucinda said as they parted at the edge of the woods."

"I'll try!" Merry waved to her friend, then plodded as quickly as she could across the yard through the deep snow. At least her aunt's car wasn't there yet. Maybe Mrs. Boggs was still asleep.

But the sitter was awake and knitting when Merry slipped inside, and she frowned at her over her glasses. "My gracious, Meredith! What in the world were you doing out there? You'll catch your death in this cold."

Merry tugged off her boots and hung her coat in the closet. "Making a snow elephant," she said. "Wanna see him?"

Mrs. Boggs sighed as she rose slowly to her feet and followed Merry to the kitchen window. "Why, so you have—and a good one, too! Whatever made you think of that?"

Merry smiled. "It was just an idea," she said. She didn't dare tell Mrs. Boggs about going to Lucinda's. Merry knew her aunt wouldn't want

her leaving the yard to visit someone she didn't
know, but the thought of not seeing Lucinda
again was just too awful to think about.

That night Aunt Martha made waffles for
supper and Meredith ate two with warm maple
syrup.

"It's good to see your appetite come back,"
her aunt said, smiling. "Mrs. Boggs says you've
been outside in the snow."

Merry nodded. She wanted to tell her aunt
about Lucinda but what if Aunt Martha were to
forbid her to visit her friend? Lucinda, Merry
decided, would have to be her secret for now.

"I'll try to get home a little earlier tomorrow
so we can go and get our tree," Aunt Martha
said when she came in to read to Merry that
night.

Merry hoped she wouldn't come home too
soon.

Chapter Seven

That night Merry dreamed she and her mother were sitting together in the rope swing that used to hang from the big oak tree behind their house. Merry sat in her mother's lap as she did when she was small, and as they swung, her mother sang a song Merry had almost forgotten:

Up and down, round and round, all the way to Boston town,

Up and down, round and round, to buy little

The Christmas Cottage

Merry a blue silk gown!

The color of the gown changed with every verse, and Merry thought the song was written just for her. She woke up smiling.

Her dad hadn't telephoned the night before, which, Aunt Martha said, probably meant her mother was the same. But Merry had a feeling her mother knew she was thinking about her, even though she was still in her deep sleep.

That afternoon when Mrs. Boggs dozed off, Merry put on her wraps and hurried outside where Lucinda waited at the edge of the yard. The snow had frozen during the night and the icy crust crunched when they walked. In a clearing across from Lucinda's brown cottage, the snow sloped away in a gentle hill and the two took time about sliding in a large cardboard box. When the box fell apart, they went down on their backsides, laughing, rolling and tumbling, until Merry felt cold clean through.

"You look like a snowman!" Lucinda said, brushing herself off after diving into a deep drift. Her breath made clouds when she spoke.

"I feel like one," Merry said, shivering.

"I feel like making fudge!" Lucinda slapped her mittens together. "Race you to the house!"

The warmth of the little house enfolded them as soon as they stepped inside, and when they had dried themselves by the fire, Lucinda's mother let them help crack pecans and pick out nut meats for the fudge. Merry and Lucinda ate as many as they saved, but when they finally had enough, she showed them how to stir together the chocolate, sugar and milk, then cook it to make the rich candy. It was dark and creamy and smelled wonderful. Merry thought it was the best she had ever eaten.

When the baby woke from his nap, he smiled and held out his arms, and Lucinda's mother let Merry rock him in a big soft chair by the fire. The baby laughed as Merry sang the "Boston" song while they watched bright embers fly up the chimney. The mantel was covered with evergreens and clusters of crimson berries and the big tree in the corner glimmered with what seemed like hundreds of star-like lights. She nuzzled the baby's downy hair and kissed his soft cheek. Merry wished she had a baby brother just like him!

"It's supposed to snow again tonight," Lucinda said later as they walked back down the trail together. "If you come earlier tomorrow, we can make snow ice cream."

"Maybe Mrs. Boggs will go to sleep sooner if I sing to her," Merry said, and they laughed.

Mrs. Boggs! What if she was already awake? What if Aunt Martha was home? Merry remembered what her aunt had said about leaving work early to get a tree.

"Gotta hurry! See you tomorrow—I hope!" she called, and plunged ahead, half sliding, half running across the frozen snow.

Her aunt was turning into the driveway and blew her horn when she saw her.

"Meredith! What are you doing out here—making another snow animal? And where's Mrs.

Boggs?" Aunt Martha pulled up in a flurry of ice and snow.

"Oh, it's okay . . . she's inside." *Think fast, Merry!* "I thought I'd see if I could find something green for the mantel."

"Well, we can do that tomorrow. Run in now and tell Mrs. Boggs we'll give her a ride home. I'd like to get back with our tree before it starts to snow again," her aunt said.

Merry almost slipped in the snow as she hurried inside to wake Mrs. Boggs and tell her they were leaving. She hoped her aunt wouldn't change her mind and come inside to find the sitter had been asleep. Sleeping was the best thing Mrs. Boggs did, Merry thought. But Mrs. Boggs was getting her knitting together, having been awakened, no doubt, by the sound of Aunt Martha's car.

The tree was a fat, short one and Merry helped her aunt put it in the stand by the window. Aunt

The Christmas Cottage

Martha had bought new ornaments—all the same color. Merry thought the tree looked kind of boring, but it smelled nice, and the colored lights winked green and red in the firelight.

"Now, we'll have to see about putting some presents under there," Aunt Martha said. She had picked up makings for sandwiches on the way home, and the two ate in the kitchen as Christmas music played on the radio. Merry wondered what Buddy was doing now and thought of Ginny sitting at a big table at her grandparents' house with all her cousins around. Then she thought of her mother quiet and still in a hospital bed miles away, and the bite of bread and meat had a hard time going down.

Aunt Martha put down her sandwich. "Oh, I almost forgot! Some letters were in the box for you today, I think I put them in my purse." Her aunt left the table and came back with two envelopes that she laid beside Merry's place. One was a Christmas card from Ginny who said she was having fun but missed her lots and lots.

The other was from her brother.

"It's from Buddy," Merry said. She could tell her aunt was curious. "He says he's been sledding twice and they went to see a funny movie. He and Alex were going shopping today."

"I wish there were more for you to do out here," Aunt Martha said. "I'm afraid it must be lonely for you, Merry." She reached for Merry's hand. "How would *you* like to go shopping one night? If you'll make a list, we'll see what we can do."

She didn't need to make a list, Merry thought. There was only one thing she really wanted, and she was sure her dad and Buddy felt the same. "That's okay. I like it here—really," she said to her aunt. But of course she couldn't tell her why.

Aunt Martha was on chapter six of *The Five Little Peppers* when the telephone rang that night, and Merry, curled on the couch in her pajamas, clutched Jo-Jo to her chest and buried

The Christmas Cottage

her face in Stuffy, Jr. It was about the time her dad usually called, and her aunt seemed to be on the phone longer than usual. Merry was almost afraid to look up when she heard her come back into the room.

But one look at her aunt's face told her the phone call had been good news. Her mother had awakened from the coma!

Chapter Eight

Merry could hardly wait to tell Lucinda her wonderful news, and she thought Mrs. Boggs would never nod off so she could slip away. She watched as the knitting drooped lower and lower on the woman's lap and her head sank onto her chest. A couple of hairs on the sitter's chin waved in the breeze of her snoring, and Merry was free!

It had snowed a few inches more during the night and a snowball hit her just as she stepped from the yard. Merry saw Lucinda's purple-clad figure behind a holly tree, heard the chime of her laughter.

"Wait! I have something to tell you!" she called as her friend ran ahead. But Lucinda wanted to play.

Snowballs flew as the two of them scampered through white-blanketed woods, dodging behind trees, chasing one another beneath tent-like evergreens until Merry had to stop to empty snow from her boots. "Time out!" she called, her breath coming fast.

"Okay. Truce!" Laughing, Lucinda plopped down beside her and did the same. "Now, what was that you wanted to tell me?"

"My mom has come out of her coma," Merry told her. "Dad called last night. She even sat in a chair for a while."

"Oh, I knew it! I just knew it!" Lucinda's gray eyes sparkled. "What wonderful news!" She threw her arms around Merry, managing in the process to slip snow down Merry's back, and that, of course, resulted in another chase.

The two paused now and then to slide down a tempting slope, or watch a squirrel leap from limb to limb above them. Once they came upon a crooked tree with a hollow near the roots where Lucinda said elves lived.

"How do you know?" Merry asked, wanting to believe.

"I think they come and go through that little hole in the roots. That's probably their door. Look," Lucinda said, "you can see tiny footprints."

Merry thought they looked like a rabbit made them, or maybe a squirrel, but it did look awfully like the kind of tree elves might live in. "Let's hide and watch for them," she said.

And so they did—until Merry's stomach rumbled and she thought of the snow ice cream her friend had promised.

Today a garland of feathery hemlock twined through the fence around Lucinda's cottage, and a bell rang light and clear when they opened the gate. Merry didn't even wait to take off her coat before sharing her news with Lucinda's mother.

"What a happy Christmas present!" her friend's mother said, gathering both girls into her arms. "This calls for a party, I think." Even the baby laughed and clapped his hands to join in the celebration.

Lucinda's mother set a pan of cooked custard to cool in the snow, and while it was cooling, the three of them rolled out sugar cookies, then cut them in shapes of stars, bells, trees, and angels for the girls to decorate with colored sprinkles. When the cookies were done, Lucinda's mother said the custard should be cool enough to make snow ice cream. She put a little of the custard in the bottom of each girl's bowl and showed them how to add the snow a little at a time until it was just the right consistency. It was so good, Merry tried to eat it too fast and thought her throat would freeze! She wished she could take a few of the sweet, crisp cookies to share with her aunt, but then she would have to explain where she got them.

Lucinda gave the cat a tiny taste of the ice cream while Merry played on the rug with the baby. A bowl of rosy apples sat on a table by the fire and the Christmas tree twinkled in its glow. Merry thought of Aunt Martha's tree, which wasn't nearly as pretty—but that didn't seem to matter any more.

When Lucinda asked if she wanted to play a game, Merry said she thought it was time she started back. Even though it was too early for her aunt to get home, Merry wanted to be there in case her dad should call.

And call he did—but the phone didn't ring until Merry and her aunt were finishing supper.

"Someone wants to talk with you," Aunt Martha said, smiling as she handed Merry the receiver.

Merry could hardly believe it when she heard her mother's voice! It was little more than a whisper, but it was her mother just the same and it sounded like a lullaby to Merry.

Her mother said she loved her and missed her and hoped to see her soon. Merry could tell she was crying a little. Merry cried, too.

"Your dad says your mom's eating better now and even took a few steps with a little help today," Aunt Martha told her. "She still has her shoulder in a cast and a brace on her leg; we can't expect her to jump up and dance for a while, but it sounds like she's on her way back!"

"When will I be able to see her?" Merry asked.

Her aunt just smiled. "I don't know, Merry . . . but if all goes well, then maybe sometime soon."

Aunt Martha said she thought Merry's mom would probably feel like reading before very long, and might like some books for Christmas. "And what about a pretty throw?" she suggested. "Something to keep her warm and snug while she's resting? Maybe we can do a little shopping tomorrow."

Merry thought that was a good idea. Earlier, in Brownie Scouts, she had made her mother a terra cotta ornament. Using Christmas cookie cutters, the troop had cut the figures from clay, then their leader had them fired in a kiln. Merry had made a snowman and an angel, only the tip of the angel's wing broke off in the kiln, so she gift-wrapped the snowman for her mother and hid it away for Christmas in the drawer where she kept her bathing suits.

The angel was still in Merry's book bag, and the next morning she took it out and looked at it. The wing was barely chipped, Merry thought, and if you didn't know it was broken, you might not even notice it. Lucinda and her mother had been so nice to her, she wanted to give them something, and Merry was sure they wouldn't mind if the angel's wing wasn't perfect.

Mrs. Boggs gave her a length of green yarn to string through the ornament, and Merry wrapped it in bright red tissue and tied it with a yarn bow.

Chapter Nine

"I've brought you something for your tree," Merry said to Lucinda and her mother the next day, as she slipped the small package from her pocket.

Lucinda unwrapped it eagerly. "Oh, look! It's an angel! How pretty! Thank you, Merry. Did you make this?"

"Our Scout leader helped us make them, and I wanted you to have it," Merry said. "I'm afraid the end of her wing got broken."

"But that just makes her even more special," Lucinda's mother said, dangling the ornament in her fingers. "Why, you could even wear it as a necklace!" and she laughed as she draped the terra cotta angel around her daughter's neck.

Lucinda wore the angel while they covered large pine cones with suet and bird seed to hang on the big cedar tree by the gate. "A Christmas present for the birds," Lucinda said, as she and Merry tied the cones onto snow-covered limbs with bright red ribbons.

And later, she wore it as she danced with the cat while her mother played carols on the piano.

Merry had told them about her mother's phone call and that her aunt was taking her shopping, and Lucinda decided that "Joy to the World" would be just the right song to sing—and so they did.

"What's your favorite carol, Merry?" Lucinda's mother asked as the two sat on the piano bench together, with Merry holding the baby in her lap.

"I like 'Silent Night' the best," Merry said, and sang it softly while the Lucinda's little brother rested against her shoulder.

"It's my favorite, too," Lucinda said, joining her.

Merry looked about her at the fire-lit room, the kind friends, the sweet-smelling baby, and the words of the old carol nestled and bloomed in her heart.

Lucinda was quiet as she walked with Merry down the trail for home that day—past the tree with the pine cones in it, the slope that was good for sliding, the hollow oak where elves lived. And when Aunt Martha's house came in sight, her friend reached out and gave her a hug. "Don't forget how to make a snow elephant," she said, then gave Merry a kiss on the cheek before turning back down the wooded road.

"I won't," Merry said after her, but she thought it was a strange thing to say. How could she forget how to make a snow elephant with Lucinda there to remind her?

"See you tomorrow!" she called. But Lucinda didn't answer.

Chapter Ten

While Mrs. Boggs was making herself a cup of tea, Merry crept quietly past her, and down the hall to her room. Soon, Merry hoped, she would be able to tell Aunt Martha of her friendship with Lucinda and her mother.

And that time came sooner than she expected.

The telephone was ringing when Merry and her aunt returned from shopping that night. Aunt Martha raced inside to answer it, with

Merry, her arms full of packages, trailing closely on her heels. She knew the call must be from her dad, and her heart thudded so hard, she thought it might break her breast bone! She was relieved to see her aunt's face break into a huge smile.

"That's wonderful!" Aunt Martha exclaimed, reaching for Merry's hand. "Well, of course I will! I'm due some time off anyway . . . I'll try to arrange things in the morning so we can be away by noon."

Merry's mother was coming home! The doctor had said that if she had someone to stay with her for a week or so until her strength returned, he would dismiss her from the hospital.

"Now, your mother will still need rest and quiet," Aunt Martha warned. "And the rest of us will have to help keep the house running smoothly, but it looks as though we'll all be together for Christmas!"

Merry grabbed her aunt about the waist and the two of them danced around the kitchen and into the living room until they collapsed on the sofa, laughing. She was so excited, Merry thought she would never get to sleep that night. Christmas was three days away—and she was going home!

Aunt Martha spent a lot of time on the phone the next morning telling Mrs. Boggs and others of their plans and arranging time off from work, and then of course they had to pack. Merry's suitcase was ready in minutes, but her aunt had to decide what clothing of her own to take—as well as the gifts they planned to bring.

"I'd like to get there in time to go to the grocery store," Aunt Martha said later as she tucked the last of their luggage into the trunk of her car. "Your dad has ordered a turkey and he said the neighbors are bringing food, but I want to be sure we have what we need for the holidays."

She glanced at Merry who hesitated on the

snow-covered walk. "Well, come on, honey. Aren't you ready? We want to get there before dark." Aunt Martha opened the passenger door and waited.

Merry looked back at the snow elephant, whose trunk was beginning to sag a little. "I have to tell my friends goodbye," she said.

"Friends? What friends? Meredith, this is no time to be funny. We have to get on the road." Her aunt still stood there holding open the car door.

"They live in the woods—just down the road back there. Please! It won't take long!"

Shrugging, Aunt Martha closed the passenger door. "Merry, there is no road back there. Show me what you mean."

Merry thought it was a good thing they were both wearing boots as she led the way past the snow elephant to the edge of the woods where the trail should begin.

Behind her, her aunt stamped her feet in the snow. "I don't see any trail. Nobody lives back here, Merry. I think it used to be a logging road, but you can see it's grown up now."

"But it's here! *They're* here! I saw them just yesterday." Merry peered into the bleak winter woods. Trees and bushes grew where the road had been, and try as she may, she couldn't see the path.

Aunt Martha stooped beside her. *"Who's* here, Meredith? Nobody lives in these woods—never have that I can remember."

Merry began to cry. "Lucinda lives there. Lucinda and her mother . . . and her baby brother, too. They live in a little brown house."

"Lucinda who?" her aunt wanted to know. But Merry didn't answer because she didn't know.

Aunt Martha cupped Merry's face in gloved hands. "Merry. I think you might have imagined your friends. I know it's been lonely here for you, and you were worried about your mother . . . but there is no Lucinda back here—no little brown house."

"There is! There is!" Merry broke away from her aunt's touch and began to run in what she thought was the right direction. In places the snow came over her knees, and once she tripped over a log and fell facedown in the snow. Was it the log where she had seen the rabbit? "Lucinda!" Merry called. "Lucinda, where are you?" But nobody answered.

She could hear her aunt calling behind her, but Merry plunged on. The little brown house was here. It *had* to be here somewhere!

Farther along she saw the crooked oak with the hollow trunk. The elf tree! It couldn't be much farther now . . . and there was the slope where they had gone sliding! Hearing her aunt closer now, Merry waited to show her.

"This is where Lucinda and I slid down the hill on boxes," she told her. "And just ahead, on the other side of that pine, is their house. You'll see . . ."

The big cedar stood near where the fence had been, but the fence wasn't there. The house wasn't there. Merry looked to see if there were pine cones in the cedar—Christmas gifts for the birds. Nothing.

Merry looked up at her aunt. "There was a house right here. It had a wreath on the door and candles in the windows . . ."

"Merry . . ." Her aunt spoke softly. "Honey, don't you think you might have dreamed it?"

No. She knew she hadn't dreamed it. The brown house—Lucinda's house—had nestled right here in the cup of these hills with snowcapped trees like arms around it. And now it was gone.

Merry closed her eyes. When she opened them again, the house would be there and she would see Lucinda again. But it wasn't and she didn't. Merry took her aunt's hand. "I don't know," she said. "Maybe."

Chapter Eleven

". . . Are you all right?" The voice seemed familiar. Warm and comforting. Merry wanted to pull the words over her like a downy blanket and go back to sleep.

Someone touched her on the shoulder. It was the hospital volunteer who had been sitting across from her earlier. Merry opened her eyes in the predawn darkness of the small chapel. Her throat felt dry and she had a crick in her neck from resting against the back of the pew.

The Christmas Cottage

How long had she been asleep?"

"Do you know what time it is?" Merry squinted to look at her watch. What if someone had tried to find her?

"A little after five—it's early yet." The woman in gray sat beside her. Had she been here all night, too?

Merry rubbed her neck. "I didn't mean to stay—guess I slept through most of the night." She stood abruptly. "I have to hurry! My husband's in ICU—they won't know where to reach me."

The woman spoke softly. "They would page you if anything changed. Why don't we check with them and see? But I doubt if they'll let you in before six."

Silently, they walked up the aisle together and took the elevator to the third floor. Neither spoke, but Merry sensed the other's concern. Had this person been assigned to her as some kind of shepherd? Whatever the reason, Merry was glad of her presence.

MIGNON BALLARD

The nurse with the snowman earrings was drinking coffee.

"I'm Meredith Enright," Merry said, parting the poinsettias. "My husband, Brian, is he . . . ? You haven't been trying to page me, have you? I'm afraid I fell asleep in the chapel."

The nurse put down her cup and wrote something in a folder. "I haven't heard them page you, and I've been here all night." She smiled. "I hope you got some rest. Why don't you go and freshen up a bit?" She glanced at the clock. "Only forty-eight minutes until they open the doors."

Forty-eight minutes! It might as well be forty-eight hours, Merry thought as she dashed water on her face and brushed her teeth. She wondered if Brian would recognize her today, and prayed that the super antibiotic dripping into her husband's veins would bring him back to her. She took time to run a comb through her hair and added a touch of lipstick, but it didn't make her feel any better.

The Christmas Cottage

The waiting room was still dark, and outside a steady rain fell. Merry's spirits fell with it. How was she going to get through this alone?

"I've brought coffee." The volunteer in gray stood in the doorway of the snack room with a thermos in her hand. "That stuff you get from the machine is awful, and there's plenty here for both of us."

"Oh, thank you! I'd love some." Merry accepted a cup gratefully and took a long swallow. The coffee tasted of cinnamon, and she could feel it reviving her sip by sip. Her companion sat by the shadowy doorway, but Merry couldn't sit still. "I don't think I can stand to wait another forty minutes," she said, pacing to the window.

"I believe I know something that will help." The Gray Lady set her cup aside. "Follow me."

"Oh, I can't—shouldn't. What if they call? I want to be here when the doors open." Merry drank the last of her coffee and tossed the paper cup into the trash.

"You will be, I promise. And this is just one floor up." She put a gentle hand on Merry's arm. "There's plenty of time. You'll be glad you went."

The fair-haired woman wore a crisp white apron over her gray uniform and her eyes were about the same color as her dress. Serene eyes that gleamed with humor—and something else. Wisdom?

And she had been so kind . . . Merry didn't want to be left alone. "All right," she said, following her. "But only for a minute."

"You must have been in the chapel all night," Merry said as they rode up on the elevator. "Do you have someone here, too?"

The woman smiled. "Oh, yes."

Lights were brighter on the fourth floor, and people bustled about. Somewhere a baby cried. Merry trailed the Gray Lady down the corridor and around a corner where her companion tapped on a glass partition, then waited until someone opened the shades. Merry stepped closer and sighed. Babies!

One tiny, red-faced boy kicked and cried lustily as a nurse gave him a bath. A dark-haired infant, wrapped in a pink blanket, was being rocked, another having her diaper changed; two babies slept. Merry smiled, feeling ten pounds lighter. Their own new grandbaby was due any time now—hers and Brian's. She might even be born this very day!

"Babies and Christmas. They go together, don't they?" Merry whispered. "I was a Christmas baby, you know."

"We're all Christmas babies," the woman answered quietly.

Later, they stood together outside the doors of the intensive care unit with a knot of worried, sleepy people who had but one thing in common: a loved one in the ICU. Merry felt a kinship with them as they waited there together, and she was glad of the kind volunteer who kept her from being alone.

"Are you coming in?" she asked her friend as the heavy doors buzzed open, but the woman smiled and shook her head. "You'll be just fine."

Charles, the nurse with the gold earring was gone, but another had taken his place. Andy was clean shaven and burly with gentle brown eyes and a soft voice. "Mrs. Enright?" he said, holding out his hand. "Somebody wants to see you."

"Well, he's come round the bend," Dr. Pierpont said later as they spoke together in the hallway. "Frankly, last night I wasn't so sure of his chances, but we're lucky. Your husband's going to be fine."

He was a small man with a trim mustache and tiny gold-rimmed glasses, and if Merry wasn't afraid she would scare him to death, she would've hugged him then and there. Her husband had a long recuperation ahead of him and would probably need physical therapy for a while, the doctor told her, but in a week or so he hoped to be able to move him closer to home.

Merry spent the next hour calling their children to tell them the good news. She also phoned her husband's business associate, Walker Langford, and thanked him for getting Brian to the hospital so quickly. And then, of course, she had to find a place to stay close by. Fortunately, the Gray Lady who had befriended her, had mentioned an affordable place to board only a couple of blocks away.

Merry had become so caught up in the excitement of her husband's calling her name, and even whispering that he loved her before dropping back to sleep, that she hadn't thought to look for the woman who had been so kind to her.

The curly-haired nurse with the snowman earrings was getting ready to go off duty when

Merry approached the desk. "Can you tell me
where I might find the Gray Lady who was here
earlier?" she asked. "She was with me most of
the night and I never had a chance to thank
her."

"Gray Lady?" The nurse shrugged into her
coat, collected her things together.

"The hospital volunteer. Fairly tall with
blond hair. She helped me through a pretty
rough night."

"Our volunteers wear pink uniforms, and
they're never here at night," the woman said.
"But someone did leave a message for you
earlier, and now that you mention it, I believe
she was wearing gray. Had a little clay pendant
around her neck—an angel, I think."

With a broken wing. Merry smiled. "What
did she say?"

The nurse shrugged. "Didn't make any
sense to me, but she wanted me to ask if you
remembered how to make a snow elephant."

MIGNON BALLARD is the author of fifteen books, including *Aunt Matilda's Ghost*, an award-winning mystery for young readers, and *The War in Sallie's Station*, a novel for adults telling of a young girl's bittersweet coming of age in time of war. Other works are: *Raven Rock, Cry at Dusk, Deadly Promise, The Widow's Woods, Final Curtain*, and *Minerva Cries Murder*, as well as *Bandstand Tales* and *Bandstand Tales II*, musicals based on the history of Fort Mill, S.C.

Her Augusta Goodnight Mysteries include: *Angel at Troublesome Creek, An Angel to Die For, Shadow of an Angel, The Angel Whispered Danger, Too Late for Angels*, and *The Angel and the Jabberwocky Murders*. The seventh in the series, *Hark the Herald Angel Screamed*, is due from St. Martin's Minotaur in the fall of 2008.

Born and reared in Calhoun, Ga., Mignon and her husband live in Fort Mill, S.C., where she wraps herself in Christmas every year as soon as the first carol is played.

Visit her website at www.mignonballard.com.

Printed in the United States
200884BV00017B/105/A